Time of Wonder

TIME
of WONDER

By ROBERT McCLOSKEY

THE VIKING PRESS · NEW YORK

Time of Wonder

Out on the islands
that poke their rocky shores
above the waters of Penobscot Bay,
you can watch the time of the world
go by, from minute to minute,
hour to hour, from day to day,
season to season.

You can watch a cloud peep over
the Camden Hills, thirty miles away
across the bay—see it slowly grow
and grow as it comes nearer and
nearer; see it darken the hills with
its shadow; and then, see it darken,
one after the other, Islesboro,
Western Island, Pond Island,
Hog Island, Spectacle Island,
Two Bush Island—darken all
the islands in between, until

you, on your island, are standing
in the shadow, watching the rain
begin to spill down
way across the bay.

The rain comes closer and closer.
Now you hear a million splashes.
Now you even see the drops
on the water...
on the age-old rocky point...
on the bayberry...
on the grass....
Now take a breath—

IT'S RAINING ON *YOU!*

At the water's edge on a foggy morning in the early spring you feel as though you were standing alone on the edge of nowhere.

You hear a snorting sound from out of the nowhere and you know that no, you are not alone. A family of porpoises is nearby, rolling over and over, having an acrobatic breakfast of herring under the bay.

Then through the fog you hear Harry Smith over at Blastow's Cove start the engine of his lobster boat and go out to pull his traps.

Suddenly there is a ripple and a splash along the shore that makes you jump! It is the wake from Harry Smith's lobster boat, and you smile because you almost got wet feet that time!

The ripple disappears into the fog, and though you cannot see it you know that it is silently gliding, gliding on its way. Then another distant, unseen splash—and the gulls and cormorants on Two Bush Ledge, with their seabird sense of humor, start giggling and laughing because they too were suddenly surprised by the wake.

Back from the shore
the trees look like ghosts.
The forest is so quiet
that you can hear an insect
boring a tunnel deep inside a log.
And that other sound—
not the beating of your heart,
but the one like half a whisper—
is the sound of growing ferns,
pushing aside dead leaves,
unrolling their fiddle-heads,
slowly unfurling,
slowly stretching.

Now the fog turns yellow.
The bees begin to buzz,
and a hummingbird hums by.
Then all the birds begin to sing,
and suddenly

the fog has lifted!
And suddenly
you find that you are singing too,
  With the blue water sparkling
    all around, all around,
  With the blue water sparkling
    all around!

At the height of the summer season the bay is spotted with boats— with racing sailboats, with cruising schooners, with busy fishing boats, and with buzzing outboards.

In the afternoon you sail among the islands, pushed by gentle breezes. You sail close by Swain's Cove Ledges, where a mother seal is nursing her baby.

And then at sunset, with porpoises puffing and playing around your boat, you come about and set a course for the island that is home.

The rock on the point of the island is very old. It was fiery hot when the world was new. It was icy cold when a glacier covered it with grinding weight.

This morning the rock is warm in the sun, and loud with happy noise of children who have come to spend the day.

They dive off the rock and swim, then stretch out, dripping, in the sun, making salty young silhouettes on the old scars made by the glacier.

In the afternoon, when the tide is out, they build a castle out of rocks and driftwood below the spot where they had belly-whoppered and dog-paddled during the morning.

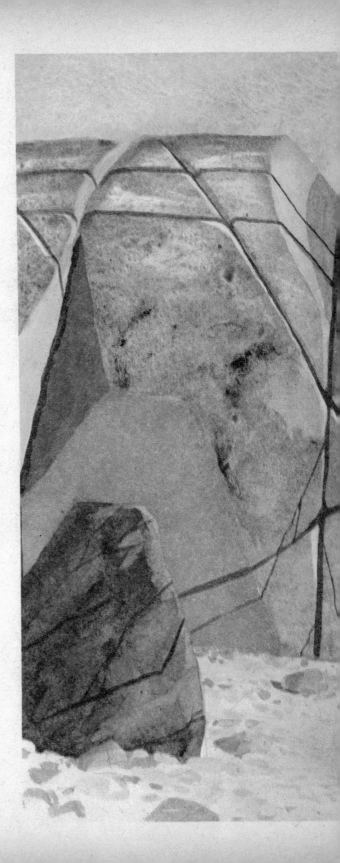

In the evening,
when the tide is high again,
and all your guests have gone,
you row around to the point,
feeling lonely,
until an owl asks a question.
A heron croaks an answer.

A seal sniffs softly as he recognizes
you, and eider ducks and fishhawks—
all are listening, all are watching
as you row. By the rock, you shine
a light down into the water.
There is a crab on the bottom
where you were playing
this afternoon.

He tiptoes sideways
through the castle gate
and disappears
into its watery keep.

You snap off the light
and row toward the dock
as the stars are gazing down,
their reflections gazing up.
In the quiet of the night
one hundred pairs of eyes
are watching you,
while one pair of eyes
is watching over all.

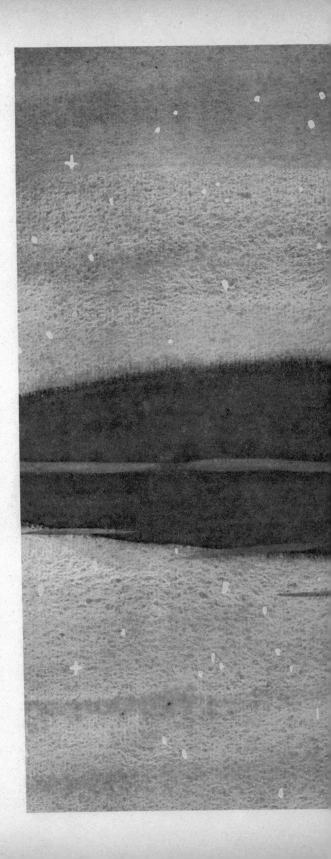

As the days grow shorter and
shorter there are fewer and fewer
boats on the bay, until at last
only the fishing boats are left.
The wind blows brisk
from the northwest, rustling
the birch leaves.

The ferns change from green
to yellow to brown. The robins are
gone from the lawn and the garden.
The swallows have flown
from their nests in the boathouse.

To take their places, migrating
birds from the north stop off to rest
on their way south. The crows and
the gulls fly over, fussing and feuding.
And the hummingbirds visit the
petunia patch.

Mr. Billings flies over, looking for
schools of herring. When he sees you
waving on the beach, he dips the
seaplane's wings in greeting.

On some days the wind is so strong
that not even the sturdy fishing boats
are out on the bay.

Now is the time for being watchful.

And other times there is not a breath
of wind to ripple the reflection of an
unusual sky.

Now is the time for being prepared.

Over in Blastow's Cove, Harry Smith
looks at the sky and says,
"We're going to have some weather."
On Eggamoggin Reach, Clyde Snowman
listens to the loons and says, "It's a comin'!"
On Cape Rosier, Ferd Clifford listens
to the sound of the bell off Spectacle Island
and says, "She's gonna blow."

On your island you feel
the light crisp feeling go out of the air
and a heavy stillness take its place.
It's time to make a quick trip
to the mainland for food and gasoline.

It's time to get ready.

We're going to have some weather.

It's a-comin'.

She's gonna blow.

In Bucks Harbor
are the cruise schooners—
the *Alice Wentworth*,
the *Stephen Taber*,
and the *Victory Chimes*—
riding at anchor to spend the winter.
Men are busy
putting out extra anchors,
pulling up skiffs and rowboats,
checking moorings,
checking chains,
checking pennants,
getting ready.

Take aboard groceries.
Take aboard gasoline.
All of the talk is of
hundred pound anchors,
two-inch rope,
one-inch chain, and
will it hold?
And the weather ... and when?
Mr. Gray strokes his chin and says,
"With the next shift of the tide."

Hurry for home,
for there's much to be done
before the tide is too low.

The ledges behind Pumpkin Island
are covered with gulls, all sitting solemnly
faced in the same direction.
There is no giggling and cackling
as your wake splashes the ledge today.
This is no time for seabird sense of humor.

    We're going to have some weather.

    It's a-comin'!

    She's gonna blow.

    With the next shift of the tide.

Home on the island, you pull in
the sailboat, chain the motorboat fast
to its mooring, pull the rowboats
high off the beach.

Mr. Smith hurries by with a
boatload of lobster traps that he has
been taking up.

Over in Swain's Cove, Mr. Billings
puts extra lines on the wings of his
seaplane.

Fishermen put extra lines on
herring boats and scalloping boats.

At Franky Day's boat yard
up Benjamin River, and at Hal
Vaughn's boat yard up Horseshoe
Creek, men are working with the
tide pulling up sloops and yawls,
ketches and motorboats;
shackling chains,
tying ropes,
making things fast,
battening down,
getting ready.

Stack the groceries on kitchen shelves.
Bring in wood to build a fire.
Fill the generator with gas.
Then take one last careful look,
while the calm sea pauses
at dead low water.
A mouse nibbles off one last stalk
from the garden and drags it
into his mouse hole.
A spider scurries across his web
and disappears into a knothole.
All living things wait,
while the first surge
of the incoming tide
ripples past Eagle Island,
ripples past Dirigo,
past Pickering,
past Two Bush Island.
The bell-buoy off Spectacle Island
sways slightly with the ripple,
tolling…
tolling…
tolling the shift of the tide.

Gently at first the wind begins to blow.
Gently at first the rain begins to fall.

Suddenly the wind whips the water
into sharp, choppy waves.
It tears off the sharp tops and slashes them
into ribbons of smoky spray.
And the rain comes slamming down.
The wind comes in stronger and stronger gusts.
A branch snaps from a tree.
A gull flies over, flying backward,
hoping for a chance to drop
into the lee of the island.
Out in the channel a tardy fishing boat
wallows in the waves, seeking the shelter
of Bucks Harbor.

A tree snaps.
Above the roar of the hurricane
you see and feel
but do not hear it fall.
A latch gives way.
People and papers
and parcheesi games
are puffed hair-over-eyes
across the floor,
while Father pushes and strains
to close and bolt out the storm.

Mother reads a story,
and the words are spoken
and lost in the scream of the wind.
You are glad it is a story
you have often heard before.
Then you all sing together,
shouting *"eyes have seen the glory"*
just as loud as you can SHOUT.
With dishtowels tucked by doorsills
just to keep the salt spray out.

The moon comes out,
making a rainbow in the salt spray,
a promise
that the storm will soon be over.
Now the wind is lessening,
singing loud chords in the treetops.
Lessening,
it hums as you go up to bed.

And the great swells
coming in from the open sea
say SH·h·h·h… SH·h·h·h… SH·h·h·h
as they foam
over the old rock on the point.
Lessening,
the wind whispers a lullaby
in the spruce branches
as you fall asleep
in the bright moonlight.

The next morning you awaken
to an unaccustomed light made by
a frosty coating of salt on all the
windows. And out-of-doors in the
gentle morning lie reminders of
yesterday's hurricane. Fallen and
broken trees are everywhere—
on the terrace, on the path—
blocking your way at every turn.
You cannot walk on familiar paths
and trails, but you can explore
the tops of giant fallen trees,
and walk on trunks and limbs
where no one ever walked before.

Then, seeking out still more places
where no one ever walked before,
you explore the jagged holes
left by roots of fallen trees.
Under an old tree by the house
you discover an Indian shell heap,
and, poking in the thousands
of snow-white clam shells,
so old they crumble at a touch,
you realize that you are standing
on a place where Indian children
stood before the coming of white men.

Now it is time for one last chore
of hauling seaweed from the beach
to fertilize the garden.
Spreading the seaweed
with its iodine smell,
you are pleased to see
that the storm-flattened sunflowers
are once more lifting faces to the sun.
And here are the hummingbirds,
humming a hymn to the morning,
making a final round
to the last of the petunias.
It is time for hummingbirds
to leave the island.

It is the end of another summer. It
is time for you to leave the island too.
Good-by to clams and mussels and
barnacles, to crows and swallows,
gulls and owls, to sea-urchins, seals,
and porpoises.

It is time to reset the clock
from the rise and fall of the tide,
to the come and go of the school bus.
Pack your bag and put in a few
treasures—some gull feathers,
a few shells, a book of pressed leaves,
a piece of quartz that came from
a crack in the old rock on the point.

And, children, don't forget
your toothbrushes.

Then "All aboard!"
and around Deer Island,
past Birch Island,
past Pumpkin Island, and
across Eggamoggin Reach,
for the last time this year.

Take a farewell look
at the waves and sky.
Take a farewell sniff
of the salty sea.
A little bit sad
about the place you are leaving,
a little bit glad
about the place you are going.
It is a time of quiet wonder—
for wondering, for instance:
Where do hummingbirds go
in a hurricane?